Dear Parent:
Your child's love of reading starts here!

Every child learns to read in a different way and at his or her own speed. Some go back and forth between reading levels and read favorite books again and again. Others read through each level in order. You can help your young reader improve and become more confident by encouraging his or her own interests and abilities. From books your child reads with you to the first books he or she reads alone, there are I Can Read Books for every stage of reading:

SHARED READING
Basic language, word repetition, and whimsical illustrations, ideal for sharing with your emergent reader

BEGINNING READING
Short sentences, familiar words, and simple concepts for children eager to read on their own

READING WITH HELP
Engaging stories, longer sentences, and language play for developing readers

READING ALONE
Complex plots, challenging vocabulary, and high-interest topics for the independent reader

I Can Read Books have introduced children to the joy of reading since 1957. Featuring award-winning authors and illustrators and a fabulous cast of beloved characters, I Can Read Books set the standard for beginning readers.

A lifetime of discovery begins with the magical words "I Can Read!"

Visit www.icanread.com for information
on enriching your child's reading experience.

To my beautiful Milo

I Can Read Book® is a trademark of HarperCollins Publishers.
Balzer + Bray is an imprint of HarperCollins Publishers.

Otter: What Pet Is Best?
www.icanread.com

ISBN 978-0-06-284512-2 (pbk. bdg.) — ISBN 978-0-06-284513-9 (trade bdg.)

19 20 21 22 23   SCP   10 9 8 7 6 5 4 3 2 1
❖
First Edition

OTTER
What Pet Is Best?

By SAM GARTON

BALZER + BRAY

An Imprint of HarperCollinsPublishers

I have lots of toys.

I have lots of friends.

I do not have a pet.

A pet is lots of fun.

I am going to get a pet.

What pet should I get?

What pet is best?

I will look in a book!

I know just the pet to get.

"I want a lion, please," I say.

"You cannot get a lion," says
Otter Keeper.

A lion is too scary.

A lion is too hungry.

A lion might eat Teddy!

"Oh no! A lion is not the pet
I should get," I say.

"I want an elephant, please,"
I say.

"You cannot get an elephant,"
says Otter Keeper.

An elephant is too big.

An elephant is too heavy.

An elephant might squash
Teddy!

"An elephant is not the pet I
should get," I say.

"I want a monkey, please,"
I say.

"You cannot get a monkey,"
says Otter Keeper.

A monkey is too loud.

A monkey is too silly.

A monkey might get Teddy
into trouble!

"A monkey is not the pet I
should get," I say.

"I want a skunk, please,"
I say.

"You cannot get a skunk,"
says Otter Keeper.

A skunk is too smelly.

A skunk is much too smelly!

"A skunk is really not the
pet I should get," I say.

I give up. I don't know
what pet I should get!

Otter Keeper gives me a hug.

"Don't worry," he says. "I

have a surprise."

I have a pet fish!

A fish is not too scary,

or too big,

or too loud,

or too silly,

or too smelly.

A fish is the perfect pet
for me!